TALES FROM THE LAND

If you want to be my friend just bend down a little, lift up the tablecloth, and crawl with me into the Land Under My Table. There we can dream up stories, have magical adventures, and meet all sorts of wonderful creatures. The only kind you will not meet are grownups, for only the young— or the young at heart—can enter the Land Under My Table.

—*Hans Wilhelm*

Copyright © 1983 by Hans Wilhelm, Inc. All rights reserved under International and Pan-American Copyright Conventions. Published in the United States by Random House, Inc., New York, and simultaneously in Canada by Random House of Canada Limited, Toronto. *Library of Congress Cataloging in Publication Data:* Wilhelm, Hans, 1945-   . Tales from the land under my table. SUMMARY: Four tales concerning a greedy giant and a clever stranger, a grouchy king and his mouse jester, a war between cabbages and cucumbers, and a bird who wishes to be more colorful. 1. Fairy tales—United States. 2. Children's stories, American. [1. Fairy tales. 2. Short stories] I. Title. PZ8.W6488Tal 1983 [E] 83-4471 ISBN: 0-394-85511-6 (trade); 0-394-95511-0 (lib. bdg.) Manufactured in the United States of America 1 2 3 4 5 6 7 8 9 0

UNDER MY TABLE

written and illustrated by

HANS WILHELM

RANDOM HOUSE 🏠 NEW YORK

6

King
Cabbage

A long time ago there lived a cruel and greedy king named King Cabbage. He was not satisfied ruling only the land of Cabbages. He wanted to rule the whole world. And so he began to wage war against the surrounding lands. King Cabbage marched boldly forward, leading his mighty army into one kingdom after another.

Soon King Cabbage's royal dungeon was filled with the kings of all the surrounding lands—all except the King of Cucumbers, whose army was large and powerful.

"I will not let a silly cucumber stand in my way!" King Cabbage shouted at his generals. Then he told them his cunning plan to conquer the Cucumbers. "Carry out my plan tonight and don't come back without their leader!" commanded the fat king.

11

That night the Cucumbers were taken by surprise. While they were sleeping peacefully, the Cabbage army quietly invaded their land and quickly defeated the startled Cucumbers. King Cabbage's sneaky plan worked.

Then the victorious Cabbage general rudely woke the King of Cucumbers and took him prisoner.

The Cabbage general took the King of Cucumbers to the royal throne room.

King Cabbage was very pleased. "No one can defeat me now. The whole world belongs to me," he boasted.

The King of Cucumbers laughed. "That's silly. Nobody can own the world," he said.

King Cabbage turned red with fury. "Chain him up and throw him into the dungeon with the others!" he screamed. Then he ordered a feast to celebrate his victory.

That night King Cabbage became ill. He groaned and tossed and turned until suddenly he fell out of his royal bed and rolled…

bump…

bump…

bumpity…

bump!

…all the way down the stairs to the cellar. His crown came clattering after him. Finally he bounced to a stop in front of the dungeon door, where he gasped his last breath.

"Hurray!" cheered the prisoners. "Someone finally beat King Cabbage!"

And do you know who that someone was? It was a tiny, hungry worm!

"He tasted just like any other cabbage," said the humble little worm as he crawled away after his delicious meal of King Cabbage.

Giant Mountain

Once upon a time, when giants still roamed the earth, there was a small village that was plundered by a giant. "Give me your coins and jewels," he roared, "or I will eat you!" The greedy giant took all of the frightened villagers' money, and great sadness fell upon the village.

Then one day a stranger came whistling down the road. He stopped at the inn for a bite to eat, and the villagers began to tell him their sad story of the greedy giant.

When the stranger finished eating, he sat back in his chair and said, "I think I can help you."

"How?" asked the villagers.

"Give me fifty gold and silver coins and I will bring back everything the giant has stolen."

At first the villagers were afraid to trust the stranger, but he was such a friendly fellow that they finally gave him their last fifty coins.

The stranger took the sack of
coins and a spade and went to the
giant's cave. He began to dig shallow
holes in the ground.

Suddenly a dreadful voice boomed,
"What are you doing on my land?"

The stranger looked up and saw
the angry face of the giant staring
down at him. The stranger smiled
calmly and said, "I'm planting silver
and gold coins."

"Why, this meadow has the finest soil in the world for growing money trees," the stranger told the giant. "Let me plant my coins in your meadow, and at harvest time we'll split the crop between us."

The giant, who had never shared anything in his life, snatched the sack of coins and vanished over the hills and into his cave.

"My plan is working!" said the stranger to himself. Then he hid in the woods and waited.

Late that night the giant returned with his huge chest of stolen coins and jewels. And he buried every single one in the meadow!

As soon as the giant left, the stranger quickly dug up all the coins and jewels.

Then he put them in a big sack and staggered back to the village.

The villagers were so happily surprised that they celebrated for days and days. And when the stranger finally left them, they rewarded him handsomely.

The greedy giant never
bothered them again,
for he was far too busy…

busy waiting for his money trees to grow. And where the giant sat patiently waiting is known to this day as Giant Mountain.

The Little Gray Bird

Deep in a forest far away and long ago
lived a little gray bird named Harold.

Each time he saw his reflection in
the water, he thought, "Why can't I
be colorful like all the other birds?"

"If I looked different, I would be special," he thought. So he tried all sorts of clever disguises to make himself special.

A nose with glasses and a mustache . . .

a bunch of grapes . . .

a mushroom cap . .

He painted his feathers . . .

and even pasted on feathers.

"Oh, dear."

polka-dot bow . . .

flamingo-leg stilts . . .

a butterfly hat.

But no matter what Harold did, he always remained a little gray bird.

One evening an old woman
heard Harold sing.

"What a beautiful voice!"
she exclaimed. "You must
be a very special bird."

"No," he said. "I'm only
a little gray bird—not beautiful
like the others."

"Do you want to be colorful
too?" asked the woman.

"Oh, yes! More than anything!"
cried Harold.

The woman chanted some magic words,
and instantly Harold's gray feathers fell
out. In their place sprouted feathers of
every color of the rainbow, and on his
head appeared a regal crown!

"I can't wait to show my friends!"
cried Harold as he flew off.

The old woman sighed sadly.

40

Indeed, Harold was now the most spectacular bird in the forest. "What a pity to hide my beauty in this dark forest," he said. "I should live where the royal family can admire me." So Harold took leave of his home and his friends and flew off to the king's palace.

As he swooped around the palace garden, the royal family looked up at him in wonder.

"What a magnificent bird!" cried the princess. "Don't let it get away. I want it!"

"Where did it go?"

"There it is!"

"Got it!"

Harold was soon caught and put in a golden cage. There he stayed . . . all alone. Each day he grew sadder and sadder.

Some days the princess would bring her friends to his cage to admire her beautiful bird. But their praise did not make Harold happy. He wanted to fly and sing. But the cage was too small to do any real flying and he was too sad to sing. The only sounds Harold made now were little peep-peeps.

One day an old woman came to the palace to sell strawberries.

"What a magnificent bird," the woman said to the princess when she saw Harold. "Does he sing beautifully too?"

"No," said the princess. "He only peeps."

"Oh, I see," said the woman. "Then you keep him for his colorful plumage."

"Yes," said the princess. "He is a joy to look at."

Suddenly Harold understood what he had to do to gain his freedom and as soon as he was alone, he did it: He plucked out all of his beautiful feathers!

When the princess returned and saw him, she had a temper tantrum and screamed, "Get that ugly bird out of my sight!"

That was exactly what Harold wanted. At last he was free again.

"My old feathers will grow back," he said. "And I don't care if they are red, green, yellow, or just plain gray. As long as I am free and can sing."

And sing he did!

Maurice, the smallest of all the subjects of King Lester the Lionhearted, had a big job. He was court jester. He had to amuse the king with funny jokes and magic tricks. This was a big job because the king was grouchy and difficult to please.

The birds who sang Maurice awake each morning were much easier to please. They were Maurice's favorite audience. They always begged him to perform for them, and after breakfast he always did.

48

He told them jokes and did
silly stunts until they rolled
with laughter.

One day the king called a meeting. "My cousin is coming to visit," he said. Then he told everyone what had to be done. "Jester, you will write a new song to welcome him."

"But, Your Majesty," said Maurice, "I don't know how to write a song and I can't sing."

"Silence!" roared the king. "You have three days. If you fail, you will never see daylight again."

While everyone was busily preparing
the palace for the royal visitor, Maurice
paced back and forth in his room. But
no song came to him.

On the third day he left his room
in search of help.

First Maurice ran through the streets of the town, asking everyone he met for help. But the townspeople all shook their heads sadly and said, "Life in town is too busy for singing. We are sorry but we can't help you."

Then he ran out of the town and into the country, where farmers were working in the fields. But the farmers couldn't help him either.

"When our day's work is done,
we are too tired to sing," they said.

Sundown came and still Maurice had no song. "What will become of me?" he sobbed.

Then he heard a voice chirp, "Why are you crying?" It was one of the birds who sang him awake each morning. Maurice told the bird his troubles.

"We can help you," chirped the bird merrily. "We know more about singing and music than anyone. Listen, I have a plan . . ."

After Maurice heard the plan, he ran lickity-split to the castle, got a tall ladder, and began to string rows of clothesline between two towers. All through the night he worked. At dawn, just as he finished tying the last knot, King Lester appeared.

"How dare you hang clotheslines on my towers! Do you want to insult our guest?" roared the king. "Guards, throw this fool into the dungeon at once!"

"No time to lose!"

"But, Your Majesty—"

"Thank goodness for the birds!"

"Woe is me!"

That morning a royal procession led the king's cousin through the castle gate, where the king welcomed him with open arms.

Then suddenly the sky grew
dark with hundreds of birds.
They swooped down and
perched on the clotheslines.

"What's going on here?"
growled the king.

"Why, how delightful!"
said his cousin. "The birds
look just like . . .

A HAPPY SONG

Put a smile on your face, a twinkle in your eye;

Feel happy in your heart like the birds in the sky.

Show your happy heart from the outside in

With a song or a whistle and a grin. Tweedle-dee-dee!

Music and lyrics by Lucy Costello.

60

. . . notes on a music scale!"
Then all together the birds burst into song. It was such a beautiful and happy song that everyone joined in the chorus —even King Lester, who was so pleased that he gave Maurice his freedom and a medal of honor.